LIFE CYCLE OF A

BUTTERFLY

LIFE CYCLES

By Kirsty Holmes

KidHaven PUBLISHING

Words that look like **this** can be found in the glossary on page 24.

Published in 2019 by
KidHaven Publishing, an Imprint of Greenhaven Publishing, LLC
353 3rd Avenue, Suite 255, New York, NY 10010

This edition is published by arrangement with Booklife Publishing.

Designer: Daniel Scase
Editor: Holly Duhig and Imogen Ramsdale

Cataloging-in-Publication Data

Names: Holmes, Kirsty.
Title: Life cycle of a butterfly / Kirsty Holmes.
Description: New York : KidHaven Publishing, 2019. | Series: Life cycles | Includes glossary and index.
Identifiers: ISBN 9781534527324 (pbk.) | 9781534527317 (library bound) | ISBN 9781534527331 (6 pack) | ISBN 9781534527348 (ebook)
Subjects: LCSH: Butterflies--Life cycles--Juvenile literature. | Butterflies--Juvenile literature.
Classification: LCC QL544.2 H65 2019 | DDC 595.789--dc23

Printed in the United States of America

CPSIA compliance information: Batch # BS18KL : For further information contact Greenhaven Publishing LLC, New York, New York at 1-844-317-7404.

PHOTO CREDITS

Photocredits: Abbreviations: l-left, r-right, b-bottom, t-top, c-center, m-middle. Front Cover – suns07butterfly, bg – Anna Grigorjeva. 1 – suns07butterfly, bg – Anna Grigorjeva. 2 – Stella Photography. 3bg – Anna Grigorjeva, 3tr – Alexandre Le Bourdais, 3mr – Hendra Xu, 3br – Galyna Andrushko. 4l – Oksana Kuzmina, 4m – Dmitry Lobanov, 4r – Pressmaster. 5l – Alliance, 5m – Elnur, 5r – Josep Curto. 6 – Kirsanov Valeriy Vladimirovich. 7 – Leena Robinson. 8 – sutipong. 9 – Sari ONeal. 10 – Sandra Standbridge. 11 – Mathisa. 12 – Kim Howell. 13 – Leena Robinson. 14 – Chik_77. 15 – Beansprout12. 16 – CHAINFOTO24. 17 – JHVEPhoto. 18l – jzero, 18m – wikipedia, 18b – 9comeback. 19tr – suns07butterfly, 19tr – PeterMooij, 19mb – wikipedia, 19mb – 9comeback. 20 – Giles Kent. 21 – Pong Wira. 22-23 – Mathisa, 23r – Lightspring. Images are courtesy of Shutterstock.com. With thanks to Getty Images, Thinkstock Photo and iStockphoto.

LIFE CYCLE OF A

BUTTERFLY

WHAT IS A LIFE CYCLE?

All living things have a life cycle. They are all born, they all grow bigger, and their bodies change.

When they are fully grown, they have **offspring** of their own. In the end, all living things die. This is the life cycle.

BEAUTIFUL BUTTERFLIES

Butterflies are flying insects. They have four large, scaly wings which can look very beautiful. They have six legs, and a special long feeding tube, called a proboscis.

Butterflies can "smell" the air with their **antennae**!

Butterflies are very good at flying. Some fly very fast, and others fly very slowly. They suck **nectar** from flowers or juice from fruit using their long proboscis.

Butterflies can live all over the world, but most like warm weather.

EXCELLENT EGGS

The eggs are stuck to the leaf using super-sticky glue made by the female.

Female butterflies lay eggs. The female will look for a safe spot, near some food, to lay her eggs. She will lay lots and lots of them.

Inside each egg, a baby butterfly – called a larva – grows. When it is time to hatch, the larva chews its way out of the shell, which it then eats for its first meal!

Butterfly eggs come in lots of different colors and shapes.

CURIOUS CATERPILLARS

When the larva has hatched, it is called a caterpillar. Caterpillars eat, and eat, and eat!

Some caterpillars eat leaves. Others eat grass, flowers, or **bark**.

Caterpillars have a hard outer layer called an **exoskeleton**. Because caterpillars grow so fast, they have to wriggle out of this layer when it gets too small, and grow a new one. This is called molting.

Caterpillars molt four or five times because they grow amazingly fast!

THE CREATIVE CHRYSALIS

The chrysalis might look very still, but a lot is going on inside!

When a caterpillar has grown (and eaten) enough, it looks for a safe, sheltered spot, and wraps itself into a chrysalis. A chrysalis is a **cocoon** that protects the caterpillar.

Inside the chrysalis, the caterpillar molts one last time and becomes a pupa. The pupa stays in the chrysalis for up to two weeks.

The pupa forms wings, legs, antennae, and a proboscis inside the chrysalis.

BRILLIANT BUTTERFLIES

The special change that happens in the chrysalis is called "metamorphosis." When it is ready, the chrysalis becomes see-through and then the new butterfly hatches!

When the butterfly first hatches, its wings will be soft and folded up. By the time it is three to four hours old, the butterfly will be able to spread its wings and fly.

LIFE AS A BUTTERFLY

Adult butterflies spend their lives looking for food and a **mate** so they can produce their own offspring.

Butterflies like to rest and enjoy the sunshine. They don't like to fly in the rain.

Some butterflies **migrate** to find warmer weather if it gets too cold.

FUN FACTS ABOUT BUTTERFLIES

- Butterflies can taste with their feet!

ACTUAL SIZE!

- The world's largest butterfly is the Queen Alexandra's birdwing. Its wings are 10 inches (25 cm) across!

- There are between 15,000 and 165,000 different types of butterfly.

- A group of butterflies is sometimes called a "flutter."

- The smallest butterfly is the western pygmy blue. Its wings are only 0.5 inch (12 mm) across.

THE END OF LIFE AS A BUTTERFLY

Most butterflies live for a few weeks, but some **species** can live for up to nine months, especially bigger butterflies.

Most butterflies die after they have mated and laid their eggs.

Butterflies also have lots of **predators** to watch out for. Wasps, birds, snakes, toads, rats, lizards, spiders, and praying mantises all eat butterflies.

THE LIFE CYCLE

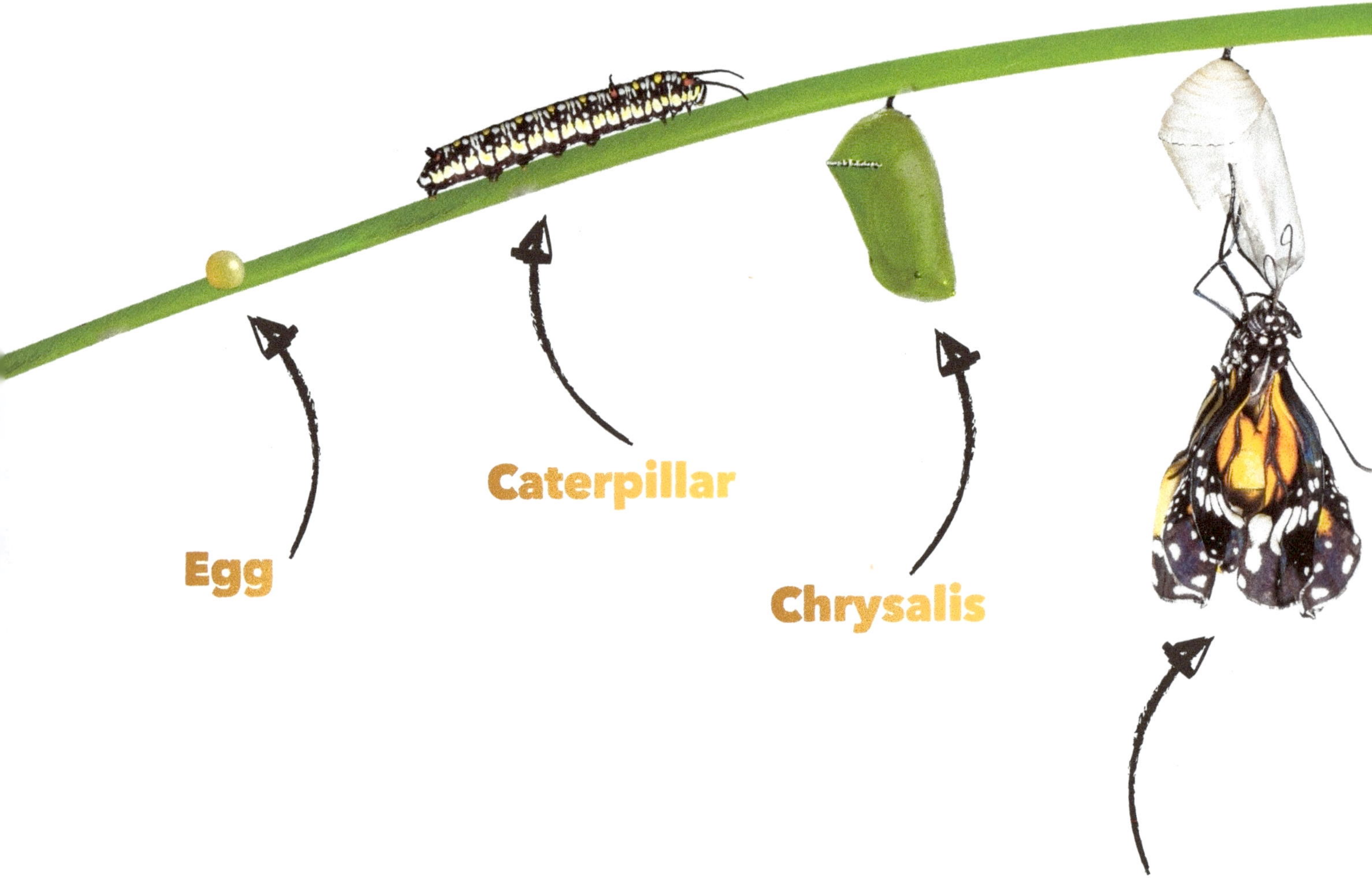

A butterfly's life cycle has different stages. All the stages are different.

The butterfly egg hatches into a caterpillar. The caterpillar makes a chrysalis and changes into an adult through metamorphosis. The adult butterfly has offspring.

GLOSSARY

antennae a pair of long, thin sensors found on the heads of insects

bark the outside cover of the trunks, branches, and roots of woody plants

cocoon a silky case spun by the larvae of many insects for protection as they change into their adult form

exoskeleton a hard structure on the outside of a creature

mate a partner (of the same species) that an animal chooses to produce young with

migrate the seasonal movement of animals from one area to another

nectar a sweet liquid made by flowers in order to attract insects

offspring the child or young of a living thing

predators animals that hunt other animals for food

species a group of very similar animals or plants that are capable of producing young together

INDEX